CLASS PLAY

Look for these
and other books
in
The Kids in Ms. Colman's Class series

Jannie, Bobby, Tammy, Sara
Ian, Leslie, Hank, Terri
Nancy, Omar, Audrey, Chris, Ms. Colman
Karen, Hannie, Ricky, Natalie

THE KIDS IN MS. COLMAN'S CLASS

CLASS PLAY

Ann M. Martin

Illustrations by Charles Tang

A
LITTLE APPLE
PAPERBACK

SCHOLASTIC INC.
New York Toronto London Auckland Sydney

ISBN 0-590-69199-6

Text copyright © 1996 by Ann M. Martin. All rights reserved. Published by Scholastic Inc. LITTLE APPLE PAPERBACKS and the LITTLE APPLE PAPERBACKS logo are trademarks of Scholastic Inc.

12 11 10 9 8 7 6 5 4 3 2 1   6 7 8 9/9 0 1/0

Printed in the U.S.A.   40

First Scholastic printing, September 1996

This book is in honor of
the birth of
Laura Caroline Hemphill

LESLIE MORRIS

"Hello, Barf-head," Leslie Morris called. She slammed the car door shut. " 'Bye, Mommy!" she said.

" 'Bye, honey," said Mrs. Morris. "See you this afternoon."

Barf-head's real name was Ricky Torres. "Hello, Stink-head," Ricky said to Leslie.

Leslie and Ricky were in Ms. Colman's second-grade class at Stoneybrook Academy. Ms. Colman was their favorite teacher. She almost never yelled, and she thought up very good surprises for her students. Everyone liked her (but most of the boys would not admit it).

Ricky followed Leslie along the walk to the entrance to school. He stepped on her heels as often as he could.

"Cut it out!" yelled Leslie.

She stopped short and Ricky ran into her.

"Ow!" he cried.

"Serves you right!" Leslie ran inside. Then she stopped and walked through the halls to her classroom. The kids at Stoneybrook Academy were not allowed to run in the halls.

Leslie stepped inside the room. She looked around. Ms. Colman was not there yet. But the door between Ms. Colman's room and Mr. Berger's second-grade room next door was open. Leslie knew Mr. Berger was keeping his eye on all the second-graders.

Only two other kids were in Ms. Colman's room. Tammy and Terri Barkan were putting things away in their cubbies.

"Hi, Terri. Hi, Tammy," said Leslie. Terri and Tammy were twins. Some days,

Leslie could not tell them apart. Today was one of those days. The girls were wearing the same outfits, and each had pulled her hair back with blue sparkle barrettes.

Leslie sat at her desk. She peered inside it. Her desk was boring. So she decided to visit Hootie. Hootie was the class pet. He was a guinea pig. He was friendly and good company.

Leslie stood next to Hootie's cage. She held Hootie in her arms. She watched her classmates arrive. Leslie decided to be the Morning Greeter. At least until Jannie Gilbert showed up. Jannie was Leslie's best friend. Leslie was never bored when Jannie was around.

"Hi, Omar!" Leslie called when Omar Harris arrived. "Hi, Ian! Hi, Chris!" she said to Ian Johnson and Chris Lamar. (The boys looked surprised to be greeted by Leslie.)

"Hi, Sara! Hi, Natalie!" cried Leslie.

Sara Ford and Natalie Springer were

trading sticks of chewing gum. "Hi, Leslie," they replied. And Sara added, "Hi, Hootie."

Next to arrive were Karen Brewer, Nancy Dawes, and Hannie Papadakis. They were best friends, just like Leslie and Jannie. They always stuck together.

"Hi," Leslie said to them.

"Hi," mumbled Nancy and Hannie. Karen did not say a word. She did not like Leslie. Or Jannie. And they did not like Karen. Or Nancy. Or Hannie. But especially not Karen.

Ricky Torres finally arrived. Bobby Gianelli and Hank Reubens were right behind him. "Hi, Barf-head. Hi, Barf-head. Hi, Barf-head," Leslie greeted them.

"Hi, Stink-head," they replied.

Soon Audrey Green arrived. Then Ms. Colman arrived. And at long last, Jannie hurried into the room.

"Where were you?" Leslie asked Jannie. She set Hootie back in his cage. "I was waiting for you."

"Sorry," said Jannie. "My dad's car would not start."

Ms. Colman clapped her hands. "Attention, please, boys and girls," she called.

It was time to start the day.

2
CLASS PLAY

Leslie ran to her desk. She plopped into her chair. Jannie plopped into hers. Jannie sat in front of Leslie. Leslie had found that she could poke the ends of Jannie's hair with her pencil, and Ms. Colman never noticed.

Ms. Colman took attendance. Then she took lunch orders. Then the kids in Ms. Colman's class listened to the principal. He made an announcement over the P.A. system.

When he was finished, Ms. Colman said, "Girls and boys, I have an announcement of my own to make."

Jannie turned around in her seat. She

grinned at Leslie. The kids loved Ms. Colman's announcements.

"Soon," began Ms. Colman, "our class is going to put on a play."

"Our whole class?" asked Chris.

"Our whole class," replied Ms. Colman. "Every one of you will be in it. And you will all help make the costumes and scenery."

"Yes!" cried Karen Brewer from the back of the room.

"Indoor voice, please," Ms. Colman reminded her.

Leslie looked around the room. Most of the kids were smiling. But not all of them. Natalie was frowning. Nancy was staring down at her hands. She looked as if she might cry.

Then Ian raised his hand. "Do we *have* to be in it?" he asked.

Ms. Colman nodded. "Yes. It will be a good experience. But most of all, I think you will have fun."

"But what if we do not want to be in the play?" asked Nancy.

"Then you will have a very small part. You will probably not even have to speak. Other kids will play the bigger parts."

"What *is* the play, Ms. Colman?" asked Leslie. She was bouncing around in her seat. She could not sit still.

"We are going to put on," said Ms. Colman, *"Alice in Wonderland."*

"Cool," said Hannie.

Leslie was still bouncing around in her seat. "Oh, Ms. Colman! Ms. Colman!" she cried. "My mother used to *direct* plays. In New York City. And I love to act."

"Wonderful," replied Ms. Colman. "I am glad you love to act because we are going to put on two performances of our play. The first one will be in the afternoon for the students and teachers here at school. The second will be in the evening for our parents and families and friends. We will use the stage in our auditorium."

Audrey raised her hand. "How will you decide who gets big parts and who gets little parts?" she wanted to know.

"Actually, I will not decide that," said Ms. Colman. "Mrs. Graff will decide." (Mrs. Graff was one of the fifth-grade teachers.) "She is going to direct the play."

"When will we get to try out for the play?" asked Hank.

"In just a couple of days," replied Ms. Colman. "And now, class, it is time for reading. Please find your books and let's begin."

On the playground after lunch that day, Leslie and Jannie sat side by side on the swings.

"I cannot wait to try out for the play," said Jannie.

"What part do you want?" Leslie asked her.

Jannie shrugged. "I don't know. I just want a good costume."

"I just want a big part," said Leslie. Then she nudged Jannie. "Pssst. There are Karen and Hannie and Nancy."

Karen, Nancy, and Hannie walked past the swings then. They did not see Leslie and Jannie. They were whispering. But Leslie heard Karen say, "I hope I get a *big* part in the play."

3

ALICE IN WONDERLAND

When recess was over, the kids in Ms. Colman's class returned to their room. They found Ms. Colman standing by her desk. She was holding up a picture book. The title of the book was *Alice in Wonderland*.

"This is not the whole story," said Ms. Colman as her students settled down. "Alice's story was told in two big books. Our play cannot tell that whole, long story. It will tell only some parts of it. Those parts are lots of fun, and full of funny characters. How many of you know the story of *Alice in Wonderland?"* Seven kids raised their hands. Nine kids did not. "Okay," Ms. Colman went on. "Today I am going to read you this short story about Alice. The play we put on will be very much like this story."

The kids in the class sat still. They listened to Ms. Colman read about the girl named Alice who fell down a rabbit hole and had wonderful adventures in an imaginary land. She changed her size, she went to a mad tea party, and she met lots of strange characters — the White Rabbit whose hole she had fallen down, the Mad Hatter, the Cheshire Cat, Tweedledum and Tweedledee, the White Queen, the Red Queen, the Mock Turtle, a Caterpillar, and even more.

"What do you think?" Ms. Colman asked, when she had finished reading.

"Cool," said Hank.

"Weird," said Bobby.

Ms. Colman smiled. Then she said, "Are you ready to see how our play will

tell Alice's story?" On Ms. Colman's desk were a pile of yellow booklets. She walked up and down the rows of kids. She gave one book to each student.

Leslie looked at her book. On the cover were the words *Alice in Wonderland*. She opened the cover. She turned the first page. She saw a list of names. It was headed *Characters*.

"Alice," Leslie read to herself. "The White Rabbit. The Cheshire Cat."

"Okay, girls and boys," Ms. Colman

went on. "Let's read through the play now. Hannie and Ian, would you read the first page aloud? Hannie, you read Alice's part, and Ian, you read the White Rabbit's part."

Hannie and Ian read. When they finished the first page, Ms. Colman said, "Do you see how the play is different from the story I just read to you? In a play, the story must be told in dialogue. That means it must be told when the characters talk to each other. It is told in conversation."

Ms. Colman asked other kids to read other parts. Leslie saw that there were plenty of parts in the play. Enough for everyone to have a role. Some of the parts, such as the Lory, were very small. (The Lory was a funny bird.) Other parts, such as the Cheshire Cat, were much bigger. The part of Alice was the biggest of all. Leslie thought of the pictures of Alice she had seen in Ms. Colman's books. Alice's hair was long and blonde. She got to wear a lovely white pinafore over a blue dress. On her feet were shiny black party shoes. Some of the other characters were quite strange-looking. The Cheshire Cat, for instance, was an enormous cat who lazed about in a tree, and often became invisible, except for his huge smile. And Tweedledee and Tweedledum — well, they were especially strange. They were fat little men wearing odd suits. The suits looked alike except that one said DEE on the collar, and the other said DUM.

Leslie wrinkled her nose. "Ew," she whispered.

"Class," said Ms. Colman, "on Thursday we will go to the auditorium. Those of you who want to try out for the larger roles may do so. The smaller roles will be assigned to the rest of you. Don't worry, there are plenty of big parts *and* small parts to go around."

Leslie frowned. She wanted only one part, and that was Alice. She looked at Karen Brewer in the back row. She just *knew* that Karen wanted to be Alice, too.

4

SPEAK UP!

On Thursday morning, Leslie felt butterflies in her stomach. As she walked down the hall to Ms. Colman's room, she leaned over and talked to her stomach.

"Go away, you butterflies," she said. "Or calm down. You are making me nervous. And I do not want to be nervous today."

"Who are you talking to, Leslie?" asked Chris as he hurried by her.

"No one," said Leslie. She felt her face turn red.

That morning Ms. Colman said to the kids in her class, "Remember, today is the day you will try out for parts in *Alice in*

Wonderland. Mrs. Graff is going to meet us in the auditorium after lunch."

After lunch? thought Leslie. That is too bad. I am going to be very nervous by then. I hope I do not barf.

Leslie did not barf. No one did. As soon as the kids in Ms. Colman's class returned from recess, Ms. Colman said, "Time to go to the auditorium. Please bring your playbooks with you."

The kids followed Ms. Colman down the hall. They sat in the first row of seats in the auditorium. Ms. Colman stood in front of them. "Girls and boys, I want you to meet Mrs. Graff," she said. "Mrs. Graff will be directing our play. That means she will be in charge of it. I will be her helper. Mrs. Graff has directed many school plays."

Mrs. Graff faced Ms. Colman's students. She was wearing a wool suit. (She looked a bit hot.) Her gray hair was combed straight down, and was neatly parted. Around her neck hung a pair of glasses on a chain. Mrs. Graff did not smile at the kids. She simply held up a playbook.

"Now. You have all read the play, so you know the story of Alice. How many of you want to try out for a part today?" she asked.

Leslie looked up and down the row. Ten kids raised their hands.

"Very well," said Mrs. Graff. "Smaller roles will be assigned to the rest of you. Okay. Let's get started. No sense in wasting time. The first role you may read for is the White Rabbit. Any of you who wishes to try out for the White Rabbit, please come to the stage now. Bring your playbooks with you."

Leslie glanced at Jannie, who was sitting next to her. "She is mean," Leslie whispered. "I don't like her."

"Me nei — " Jannie started to say.

"Girls! Shh!" said Mrs. Graff from the stage. "I expect everyone to pay attention. That is the only way to put on a play."

Leslie slumped in her seat. So did Jannie. So did several other kids.

Mrs. Graff turned to the kids on the stage. "Please open your playbooks to page four," she said. "Each of you will read the White Rabbit's lines, and I will read the other lines. Let's start with you." Mrs. Graff pointed to Hannie. "What is your name?" she asked.

"Hannie Papadakis," Hannie replied.

"Okay. Begin."

"I'm late, I'm late — "

"Speak up!" said Mrs. Graff loudly. "When you are putting on the play, people must be able to hear you in the very last row."

Hannie started over again. When she finished, the other kids read the White Rabbit's lines with Mrs. Graff. Mrs. Graff called out, "Speak up!" eleven more times.

When the kids had finished trying out for the White Rabbit, they tried out for the Cheshire Cat, Tweedledum and Tweedledee, the Mad Hatter, the Red Queen, and the other big parts. Most of the kids tried out for several parts, just in case. But not Leslie. She tried out only for Alice.

5

TWEEDLEDUM
AND TWEEDLEDEE

It was Monday morning. Ms. Colman had taken attendance. She had made some announcements. Now she sat at her desk and looked out at her students. "Class," she said, "Mrs. Graff has thought very carefully about your tryouts for the play. And she has decided who will play which parts. So get ready to listen."

Leslie squirmed in her seat. Her heart was pounding. Jannie turned around to look at her, and they grinned at each other.

"Cross your fingers," Jannie whispered.

Leslie crossed them. She crossed some of her toes, too.

"I will read your names in alphabetical order," said Ms. Colman, "and I will tell each of you which part you will play. Okay?" Ms. Colman looked at a list in her hand. "Tammy Barkan," she said. "The Lory."

Tammy groaned. She did not want to be in the play at all.

"It is a very small role," Ms. Colman told her. "You do not have to speak. Okay. Let me see. Terri Barkan, the Red Queen."

"Yes!" cried Terri.

"Karen Brewer, Alice."

Karen jumped out of her seat. "Alice? I am *Alice*?!" she cried. "Cool! Thank you, Ms. Colman! I cannot wait. I will be a great Alice!"

Hannie and Nancy clapped their hands for Karen.

Jannie turned around. "No fair," she whispered to Leslie.

"Yeah," replied Leslie. She glared at Karen. Karen thought she was so smart. She had *skipped* into Ms. Colman's class from first grade. She was always winning things and getting 100s on her quizzes. And now she was going to play Alice.

Ms. Colman was reading her list again. At first, Leslie only half listened. Jannie got the part of Tweedledum. Omar was going to be the Cheshire Cat. Chris was going to be the Mad Hatter.

Then Leslie paid attention. Ms. Colman would call her name next.

"Leslie Morris," said Ms. Colman. "Tweedledee."

Tweedle*dee*? Leslie could not believe it. She remembered the horrible picture of Tweedledee and Tweedledum in the book Ms. Colman had read. She did not want to play Tweedledee.

But Jannie was grinning at her again. "Cool! We get to be Tweedledum and Tweedledee," exclaimed Jannie. "And we are best friends, so it is perfect. We will be the best Tweedledum and Tweedledee ever."

"I guess," said Leslie.

On the playground that day, Leslie and Jannie sat on the swings. Jannie was smiling to herself.

"What?" Leslie asked her. "Why are you smiling?"

"I am thinking about the play," said Jannie. "About our being Tweedledum and Tweedledee."

Leslie made a face

"What is the matter?" Jannie asked her. She sounded cross.

"Tweedle*dee*," Leslie replied.

"Don't you want to be Tweedledee?"

"Not really."

"But I am going to be Tweedledum."

"I know." Leslie narrowed her eyes. She looked across the playground. "Stupid old Karen Brewer." Leslie waited until Karen walked by the swings. Then she

called out, "Hey, Karen! The only reason *you* got to be Alice is because you have long, blonde hair, like she does."

Karen did not say anything. She just stuck her tongue out at Leslie.

"Leslie," said Jannie, "I thought we would have fun being Tweedledum and Tweedledee."

Leslie sighed. "I am sorry, Jannie. I guess we will. It is just that I wanted to be Alice."

6
MEANIE
MRS. GRAFF

Ms. Colman smiled at her students. Then she clapped her hands together. "Okay, girls and boys. It is time for the very first rehearsal of our play. Please line up and we will walk to the auditorium."

The kids in Ms. Colman's class lined up at the door. They followed Ms. Colman down the hall to the auditorium. They found Mrs. Graff waiting on the stage.

"Okay," said Mrs. Graff briskly. "Please find seats in the front row. Natalie? That is your name, is it not? No talking while I am talking."

Silently, the kids sat down. Leslie sat between Natalie and Tammy. She looked at Jannie two seats away. She pointed to Tammy's seat.

Jannie stood up to switch places with Tammy.

"Girls," said Mrs. Graff. "I said to sit *down*."

Jannie plopped back into her seat.

Leslie sighed. She started to scowl, then stopped. She had a feeling Mrs. Graff would see the scowl. Mrs. Graff probably had eyes in the back of her head.

"All right," said Mrs. Graff. "Today I would like to work with Alice and the White Rabbit. Karen and Sara, please come up on the stage. Bring your playbooks. Ms. Colman?"

Leslie glanced at Ms. Colman, who was standing at the end of the row of kids. Ms. Colman was frowning.

"Yes?" said Ms. Colman.

"Why don't you take the rest of the students. They can start working on the scenery and costumes and props."

So Karen and Sara went onstage with Mrs. Graff. The other kids went behind the stage with Ms. Colman.

"We have a lot of work to do to get ready for the play," Ms. Colman said to her students. "But it will be fun. Together we will make the scenery for our play. And each of you will put together your own costume. Please ask me if you need help with your costumes. Your parents can help you, too, of course."

From the other side of the curtain, Leslie heard Mrs. Graff say, "You are not listening, Sara. How did I just read that line to you? You *must* pay attention."

"But I — " Sara started to say.

"No buts," said Mrs. Graff.

Leslie looked at Ms. Colman. Ms. Colman was frowning again. Maybe she thought Sara was doing a bad job.

Jannie nudged Leslie. "Mrs. Graff is a meanie," she said.

Leslie nodded.

Natalie leaned over. "I do not think Ms. Colman likes her," she said.

"Really?" whispered Leslie. Maybe that was why Ms. Colman was frowning.

Karen and Sara worked with Mrs. Graff for awhile. Then Leslie heard Mrs. Graff say to the girls, "Thank you. Remember — practice, practice, practice." She paused. "Okay," she went on, more loudly. "May I have Tweedledum and Tweedledee out here, please?"

Leslie and Jannie glanced at each other.

"Uh-oh," said Jannie.

Leslie took Jannie's hand, and they walked to the front of the stage.

"And you are . . ." said Mrs. Graff, "Jannie and Leslie?"

"I am Jannie," said Jannie.

"And I am Leslie."

"Please start reading from page twenty-six," said Mrs. Graff. "And remember to project. That means *speak up.*"

"Okay," replied Leslie. She could not wait for the rehearsal to end. Leslie had decided she hated Mrs. Graff.

7

LESLIE'S SURPRISE

The next day, the kids in Ms. Colman's class went to the auditorium. It was time for their next rehearsal.

"Everyone who is in the mad tea party scene, come to the stage," called Mrs. Graff. "The rest of you go with Ms. Colman."

Tweedledee and Tweedledum were not at the mad tea party. They went behind the stage with Ms. Colman.

"Goody," Jannie whispered to Leslie. "I do not like working with Mrs. Graff. Mrs. Graff scares me."

"Me too," said Leslie.

"Me three," said Ricky Torres.

"Shh," said Leslie. "I think Ms. Colman heard us."

Ms. Colman was frowning again.

Leslie was glad when the rehearsal was over.

That night, Leslie looked around the dinner table at her family. Her mother and father each sat at one end of the table. Leslie sat on one side. Across from her sat her sister. Barbara was eleven years old. Leslie had heard her mother say that Barbara was eleven going on sixteen. She was not sure what that meant, since everyone knows twelve comes after eleven. She *was* sure that Barbara could be a big fat pain.

Just as Leslie was taking the second to last bite of her fish, the telephone rang. Mr. Morris reached for it. But Barbara sprang out of her chair.

"Let me get it!" she cried.

"Honey — " said Mr. Morris.

"It might be Dave! Claire told Emily to

tell me that he might call tonight. And
Dave is a *boy*."

"Duh," said Leslie.

Barbara grabbed the phone. "Hello?"
she said. "What? . . . Okay, just a sec." Barbara sighed. She handed the phone to Mrs.
Morris.

"Hello?" said Leslie's mother. "Oh,
Ms. Colman. How are you?"

Barbara glared across the table at Leslie. "What did you do wrong?"

"Nothing! Nothing," said Leslie.

Leslie listened carefully to her mother. She heard her say "The play?" Then she heard her say "Mm-hmm" a lot. Finally she said, "Well, let me think it over. Let me talk to Leslie, too."

When Mrs. Morris hung up the phone, she was smiling. "Guess what Ms. Colman wanted," she said. Leslie could not guess. "She wanted to know if I would be interested in directing your class play."

"You?" replied Leslie. "But Mrs. Graff is directing it."

"I guess she cannot do it anymore. What do you think, Les?"

"Do you want to direct it?" Leslie asked her mother.

"Sure. It would be fun. But only if it is okay with you."

Leslie went to her room to think. She did not really want her mother to direct her class play. That would be almost as bad as if her mother were her teacher. Her mother would come to school every day. She would tell Leslie's classmates what to do.

That would be *so* embarrassing. What if the kids hated Leslie's mother? What if — ?

Leslie had been sitting on her bed. Suddenly, she leaped to her feet. She had just had a great idea. If her mother directed the play, then *she* would get to decide who had which parts. Just as Mrs. Graff had done. Surely Mrs. Morris would let her own daughter play Alice.

Leslie ran downstairs. "Mommy," she said, "I have been thinking. It would be great if you directed the play."

"Really?" said Mrs. Morris.

"Really," said Leslie.

Leslie smiled. Her mother would probably give out the new parts at the very next rehearsal.

8

MEANIE MOMMY

"Girls and boys," said Ms. Colman, "I have some news for you about our play."

It was the next morning. Ms. Colman was sitting at her desk. She looked around at her students.

Leslie smiled. *She* knew what Ms. Colman's news would be.

"We have a new director for our play. Mrs. Graff is very busy right now. She decided it would be better if someone else directed *Alice*. So I have asked Leslie's mother to take over. She has directed many plays."

"In New York," added Leslie.

Then Leslie turned around. She looked at Karen. She felt a little sorry for her. How sad that soon Karen would not be Alice anymore.

That afternoon, the kids in Ms. Colman's class went to the auditorium again. They sat in the first row of seats.

Mrs. Morris stood in front of them.

"Hi, kids," she said. "I am very happy to be directing your play. I know you have

already been working hard. That is great. But I want us to have some fun, too. Putting on a play should be fun."

Leslie looked up and down the row at her classmates. They did not seem to hate Mrs. Morris. (At least, not yet.) In fact, they were smiling.

"Now," Leslie's mother went on, "Ms. Colman told me you are working on the mad tea party scene. So let's start there — "

"Um, Mommy? I mean, Mom?" Leslie raised her hand.

"Yes?" said her mother.

(Leslie was glad her mother had not called her honey.)

"What about the auditions?"

"The auditions?" repeated Mrs. Morris. "You already had the auditions. The play has been cast."

"Oh. But . . . I thought you would want to start over."

"Heavens no. I am just going to pick up where Mrs. Graff left off."

"You mean I — " Leslie stopped herself. She had almost said, "You mean I cannot play Alice after all?" Instead she did not say anything.

In fact, Leslie did not say a single word until the rehearsal was over. Then she tugged on her mother's sleeve. "Mommy, can I talk to you in private?" she asked. "It is about the part of Alice. Do you think I could switch with Karen? I would really like to be Alice."

Mrs. Morris looked surprised. "Play Alice? No, honey. That is Karen's part. I already said that the play has been cast. We are not starting over."

"But — " began Leslie.

"And I meant it," said Mrs. Morris.

9

THE SNEAKY PLAN

Audrey Green raced into school. She slowed down and walked through the halls. Then she burst into Ms. Colman's room.

"Leslie, hi!" she called. "I cannot wait for our play rehearsal today!"

"Me neither!" said Sara.

Leslie scowled. Her classmates said these things every single morning now. They had never said them when Mrs. Graff was directing the play. They had been afraid of Mrs. Graff. But they loved Leslie's mother. Natalie had even said to Leslie, "You are so lucky. You get to *live* with your mother. We only see her at rehearsals."

Leslie did not think her mother was so wonderful. But she did not say so. She knew she was the only one who felt that way.

Once, just once, Leslie had asked her mother about Alice again. Her mother had smiled. She had tried to look patient. "The play has already been cast," she said to Leslie. "I told you that we were not going to start over. Karen is looking forward to playing Alice. And that," she had added, "is the end — the *very* end — of this discussion."

"Meanie," Leslie said under her breath.

Leslie found herself muttering "meanie" quite often. Mostly during the play rehearsals. And mostly when her mother was working with Karen.

The play was coming along nicely. If Leslie had not been so mad, she might have had fun. Mrs. Morris usually worked onstage with only a few kids at a time. The kids who were not onstage worked with

Ms. Colman on costumes and scenery. They painted big cardboard cups and saucers and pots for the mad tea party. They painted an enormous tree for the Cheshire Cat. They painted the room inside the rabbit hole into which Alice falls at the beginning of the play.

"Isn't this fun?" Jannie asked Leslie one afternoon.

"It is better than workbooks," said Leslie.

Jannie glanced at her. She paused.

46

Then she said, "I am almost finished with my costume. Are you? They have to look just the same, you know. Except for the DUM and DEE parts."

"I will get to mine," said Leslie.

"Did you start it yet?"

"Well, no."

"Leslie! Don't you care how we look? We have to be perfect. Our song is —"

"Stupid," Leslie muttered. She and Jannie had to sing a song together — a duet — and do a little dance, too.

"What?" said Jannie.

"Nothing."

Leslie peered between the curtains.

"Mrs. Morris?" Karen was saying. "See here in my playbook? See where it says I say this line sadly? Well, how sad should I look? This sad?" Karen looked as if she were about to cry.

"Not quite that sad," said Mrs. Morris. "I think you are more thoughtful in this scene. And maybe a little worried."

"Oh. Okay. Thanks, Mrs. Morris." Karen beamed.

"You are doing a wonderful job, Karen," said Mrs. Morris.

"Meanie," murmured Leslie.

"In fact," Mrs. Morris went on, raising her voice, "you are all doing a wonderful job. Keep up the good work."

"Meanie," said Leslie again. She looked around at her classmates. Every one of them was grinning. Leslie hoped the play was a big fat flop. She narrowed her eyes. An idea was coming to her.

"Leslie?" said Omar. "What are you thinking about?"

"Nothing," replied Leslie. This was a lie. Leslie had just thought of a very sneaky plan.

10

THE THIEF

In Ms. Colman's class, it was prop day. Each of the kids had been asked to find one or two props for the play. Karen was to find two bottles and paste a label on one that said DRINK ME, and a label on the other that said EAT ME. These were very important props for the rabbit hole.

Chris was to find a three-legged stool. That was also for the rabbit hole.

Everyone had an assignment. And everyone was supposed to bring the props to school on prop day.

"Well? How did you do?" Ms. Colman asked her students.

"Fine!" they answered.

"Did you find everything?"

"Yes!"

"But the stool was really hard to find," added Chris.

"So was this," said Hank. He held up a large brass key.

"I found lots of *four*-legged stools," Chris went on. "But not three-legged ones. Finally, my aunt let me look in her attic."

"My mom had to call an *antique* store to get the key," said Hank. "But the woman there let us have it for fifty cents."

"You have all worked very hard. I can see that," said Ms. Colman. "Thank you. We will bring our props to the auditorium today."

Good, thought Leslie. That will fit right into my plan.

That afternoon, the kids in Ms. Colman's class piled their props behind the stage. They looked at them proudly.

"My," said Leslie's mother. "You certainly have been busy. Good job." (Leslie's classmates grinned.) "All right, today I would like to see the March Hare, the King, and the Dormouse, please," Mrs. Morris went on.

"The rest of you come with me," said Ms. Colman. "You may continue working on the scenery. And I want to start checking on your costumes."

The kids rushed for the paint cans and brushes. Leslie waited until Ms. Colman was talking with Nancy Dawes. Then she wandered over to the props. She looked through them carefully. At last she saw what she wanted. The brass key. She made sure no one was watching her. Then she slipped the key in her pocket.

A few minutes later, Leslie was busily painting a large cardboard teapot. She heard a yelp.

"Hey!" someone cried. "Hey, the key is gone!"

It was Hank. He was standing by the props.

"Ms. Colman," said Hank. "I came to

check on the key, and it is *gone!*"

"Oh, I am sure it is not really gone," replied Ms. Colman. "Come on. Let's look for it."

Ms. Colman, Hank, and a few other kids looked for the missing key. Leslie watched them. She smiled to herself.

"I will never find another key like that one!" wailed Hank.

Good, thought Leslie.

Leslie peeped through the curtains at

the kids onstage. They were saying their lines. Some of them were still reading from their playbooks. Some were not. Leslie saw Karen's playbook lying on the stage. In a flash, she whisked it away and stuck it under a trash can.

The next thing Leslie knew, Karen was calling, "Hey! Where is my playbook? I need my playbook!"

Karen searched for her book. She could not find it. Finally, she had to borrow Ian's. She started to say her lines again. "Now I do not remember where to begin," she complained.

Mrs. Morris sighed. "Okay. Let's start over."

Leslie smiled to herself. She ducked behind the curtains. Everyone was busy. No one was watching her. Leslie found a bucket of red paint. She found a big brush. She stood before the Cheshire Cat's tree. She aimed the paintbrush.

"Leslie, what *are* you doing?" exclaimed Jannie.

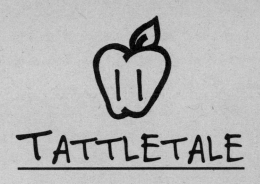

TATTLETALE

Leslie jumped. "Oh! Oh, nothing," she said. "I was not doing anything."

"Yes, you were. You were going to ruin our tree. You were going to splash red paint all over it. You hate this play. I know you do."

"So what? So what if I hate it?"

"I bet you stole Hank's key and Karen's playbook, too."

"So what if I did?"

"I am going to tell on you!"

"Go ahead, tattletale," said Leslie.

Jannie paused.

"I said, go ahead. . . . Are you a fraidy cat, too?"

"No, I am not a fraidy cat. And I am not a tattletale. But you are a big fat thief. And you are a play wrecker."

"Well, that is better than being stupid Tweedledee."

"I knew it! I knew you did not want to be Tweedledee!" cried Jannie. "Why not? Why not, Leslie? Just because you wanted to be Alice, and you did not get the part? You are so stuck up! You always have to be the best!"

"*I* am stuck up? Look who is talking. You are the one who was so mean to Karen when she skipped into second grade. You did not like her because she is younger than us."

"You were mean to her, too. And you are jealous of her!" cried Jannie.

"Well, you were jealous of Mary Washburn in first grade."

"You were the one who stole Mary's lunch. See? You were already a thief. Even back in first grade. And now you are stealing things just because you hate the play.

That is not fair to the rest of us, Leslie."

"Then maybe I will just drop out of the play."

"Good. You should."

"If I drop out, will you still tell on me?"

Leslie screwed up her face. "We-ell," she said slowly. "I don't know. Will you return the key and the playbook?"

"Yes."

"Okay. Then I will not tell."

"And I will talk to my mother tonight. I will tell her I am not going to be in the stupid play."

"Good."

"Oh, by the way. I am not your friend anymore, Jannie."

"Double good. I am not yours either."

12

MRS. GRAFF AGAIN

"Mommy?" said Leslie that night.

"What, sweetie?" replied Mrs. Morris.

Dinner was over. Barbara and Mr. Morris were cleaning up the kitchen. Leslie's mother was sitting at her desk.

"I need to talk to you," said Leslie. "About the play."

Leslie had kept her promise to meanie Jannie. She had returned the key and the playbook. (She had done those things in secret.) And Jannie had kept her promise to Leslie. She had not told on her.

"About the play?" repeated Mrs. Morris. "Okay. Come sit on the couch with me. You look upset."

Leslie did not want to look upset. At least, not too upset. She took a deep breath. She calmed down. "Mommy," she said, "I have something important to tell you. I want to drop out of the play."

"Drop out!" exclaimed her mother.

"Yes. I — I do not like playing Tweedledee."

Mrs. Morris frowned. "Hmm," she said thoughtfully. "All right. I will call Ms. Colman tonight and tell her."

"Thank you," said Leslie.

Leslie waited for her mother to call Ms. Colman. When she did, Leslie stood outside the kitchen. Very quietly, she listened to her mother's phone conversation. She knew she was eavesdropping. But she could not help herself. She wanted to make sure she did not have to be in the play.

"Hi, Ms. Colman," said Leslie's mother. "It's Mrs. Morris. I am sorry to bother you, but we have a little problem. It is Leslie. She says she does not want to be in the play anymore. She says it is because she does not want to be Tweedledee. But I think it is really because I am directing the play. I think that has been hard on her. So . . . this is very difficult for me to say, but I have to say it. I have decided not to continue directing the play. Maybe — maybe you should ask Mrs. Graff back. I have a feeling Leslie will join the play again if you do."

A long pause followed. Mrs. Morris was listening to Ms. Colman. Leslie wanted to run into the kitchen. She wanted to tell her mother that she had everything all wrong. But how could she do that? If she did, her mother would know that Leslie had been eavesdropping.

In school the next day, Ms. Colman said, "Class, I have some bad news and some good news." Ms. Colman was not smiling.

She looks as if she has all bad news, thought Ricky.

Leslie squirmed in her seat. She knew

what Ms. Colman was going to say.

"I had a long talk with Leslie's mother last night," Ms. Colman went on. "Mrs. Morris said she is very, very sorry, but she cannot direct our play any longer. Something — something came up."

Leslie could feel the other kids staring at her.

"And so," said Ms. Colman (she tried to smile), "and so Mrs. Graff agreed to take over again. Wasn't that nice of her?"

Oh, *won*derful, thought Sara.

Just fantastic, thought Bobby.

A few kids sighed. No one said a word.

"All right. Please take out your reading books," said Ms. Colman. "Natalie, may I see you for a moment?"

Leslie listened as Ms. Colman told Natalie she would be taking over as Tweedledee. "Just until Leslie changes her mind," Ms. Colman added quietly.

"But I do not *want* to play Tweedle-

dee," said Natalie. "He has too many lines."

"Just for a day or two," said Ms. Colman firmly.

Natalie shot Leslie a very dirty look.

And the rehearsal that day with Mrs. Graff was horrible.

13

TELLING
THE TRUTH

Leslie watched the rehearsal from a seat in the auditorium. Her classmates were not laughing. They were not having fun. They were not even working very hard. They just did the things Mrs. Graff told them to do.

Jannie and Natalie tried on the Tweedledum and Tweedledee costumes. Leslie thought, At least I finally brought in my costume. But Leslie's costume was too big for Natalie.

"I am going to trip in this stupid thing," said Natalie.

"Well, that is not my fault," said Jannie.

"Kids!" Ms. Colman called. "Will everyone please settle down? Natalie and Jannie, stop arguing. Hank, leave Ian alone. Nancy, that tree looks just fine. Do not worry about it." Ms. Colman heaved a huge sigh. "Mrs. Graff, I think the kids have had enough for today. We will start over tomorrow — when everyone is in a better mood."

The kids in Ms. Colman's class walked silently to their room.

"Cheer up!" said Ms. Colman.

But no one did.

Leslie could not stand it. When school ended that day, she waited by Ms. Colman's desk. "Can I talk to you?" she asked her teacher.

"Of course," said Ms. Colman.

Leslie watched the other kids leave the room. When she and Ms. Colman were alone, Leslie said, "I have something to tell you. My mother was wrong. I did not quit the play because she was the director. I quit it because I did not want to play Tweedle-dee. I only wanted to play Alice. I was mad that Karen got the part. So then I decided to wreck the play. I took the key Hank found. And I hid Karen's playbook. I was even going to ruin some scenery. The Cheshire Cat's tree. But Jannie caught me. She stopped me. She was going to tell on me, so I decided to drop out of the play instead. Only I overheard Mommy when she called you that night. She thought I dropped out because she was the director. That was not true. But I did not say anything, because then she would have known I was eavesdropping. But —"

Leslie paused. She took a deep breath. Then she went on. "But now I see how unhappy everyone is. I do not *really* want to wreck the play."

Ms. Colman had been watching Leslie. She was not smiling, of course. But she was not frowning either. At last she said, "Leslie, I am very unhappy about the things

67

you have done. I am glad you told me the truth. But you have caused a lot of problems for a lot of people."

"I know," said Leslie.

"One of those people is Mrs. Graff."

"Mrs. Graff?"

"Yes. First I asked her to be our director. Then I asked her not to be. Then I asked if she would be our director again after all. She may be strict. But she has been very patient with me."

"Hello?"

Leslie turned around to see her mother in the doorway.

"I was getting worried about you," said Mrs. Morris. "I have been waiting outside. I did not know where you were."

"Sorry," said Leslie.

And Ms. Colman said, "Leslie and I have been talking." Then she told Mrs. Morris everything Leslie had just said.

Mrs. Morris looked a lot unhappier than Ms. Colman had looked. "We will talk about this at home," she said.

"Okay," replied Leslie. "But I have to ask Ms. Colman a question." Leslie turned to her teacher. "If it is okay with you and Mrs. Graff, could Mommy be our director again? I would like her to be. And I would like to come back to the play."

"As Tweedledee?" asked Mrs. Morris.

Leslie sighed. "Yes."

14

BAD AND GOOD

For Leslie, the next few days were both bad and good.

Driving home from school after the talk with Ms. Colman was (mostly) bad. At first Mrs. Morris drove silently, looking straight ahead. Finally, she said, "Leslie, I am very disappointed in you. *And* I am proud of you. I am disappointed that you could not be a good sport about your part in the play. I am disappointed that you tried to ruin the play. And I am disappointed that you listened in on my phone call — and then let everyone believe something that was not true. However, I am proud of you for telling the truth, for asking me to direct again, and for agreeing to play Tweedledee.

"Still," Leslie's mother went on, "you are going to be punished."

Leslie almost said, "I *knew* it." But she thought better of it. Instead, she said simply, "Okay."

"No TV for a week," said Mrs. Morris. "Also, I would like you to write a note telling Ms. Colman you are sorry. You should probably tell Mrs. Graff you are sorry, too. But I will let Ms. Colman talk to Mrs. Graff. That is a bit more complicated."

"Okay," said Leslie again. No TV for a whole *week*? Monster Marathon — six monster movies in a row — began on Saturday morning. Everyone in Ms. Colman's class was planning to watch it. Leslie would have to miss it.

That night Leslie wrote her letter to Ms. Colman. She gave it to her the next morning. And that afternoon, Mrs. Morris came to the play rehearsal.

Leslie felt bad for Mrs. Graff. And she felt bad for Ms. Colman, who had had to tell Mrs. Graff that Mrs. Morris was taking over as the director — again.

But Leslie was glad that the rehearsal went very well. Nobody argued or teased or worried too much.

And Natalie said to Leslie, "Thank you, thank you, thank you! I am *so* glad you are going to be Tweedledee again. Here is your old costume. I cannot wait to put on my Dormouse costume again!" Natalie flung Tweedledee's silly jacket and goofy tie and floppy shoes at Leslie.

Leslie looked at Jannie. She was standing nearby, holding the parts to her Tweedledum costume. She turned her back on Leslie.

Leslie glanced sadly at her mother.

"Well," said Mrs. Morris cheerfully. "Speaking of costumes, guess what?"

"What?" said the kids in Ms. Colman's class.

"It is almost time for our first dress re-

hearsal. We will be performing the play in just one week, you know."

"One *week*?" cried Karen.

Half the kids in the class looked alarmed. The other half looked excited.

"Are we going to be ready?" asked Sara.

"Yes, I think so," replied Mrs. Morris. "You have found all the props. The scenery is nearly finished. Your costumes are almost ready. And you know your lines very well. After a few dress rehearsals, you should be ready to go."

Omar raised his hand. "Um, what is a dress rehearsal?" he asked.

"It is a rehearsal when we put on the entire play. You wear your costumes, we use the props and scenery, and we rehearse the play from beginning to end, every scene."

Leslie felt a flutter of excitement in her stomach.

✏ ✏ ✏

Three days later, the kids in Ms. Colman's class held their very first dress rehearsal. They found that they knew their lines better than they thought they did. Leslie was even having fun. When it was time to sing her duet with Jannie, they walked onstage hand-in-hand in their matching costumes. But Jannie refused to look at Leslie. When their song was over, she stepped away from her.

Bad and good, thought Leslie.

BRAVO!

"**A**re they out there?" whispered Bobby.

"About a million of them," Tammy replied.

"What are they doing?" asked Audrey.

"Just sitting," said Karen. "And waiting. Waiting for us."

"What if we are not ready?" asked Bobby.

"We are ready," said Audrey. "We had four dress rehearsals."

"At the last one, the Cheshire Cat's tree fell over," said Tammy.

"Well, that will not happen today," said Karen firmly. "Not during our very first performance."

"Kids!" Ms. Colman whispered loudly. "Come away from the curtain. It is almost time for our play to begin. Please find your places. And make sure your costumes are ready."

Leslie took one peek out at the audience before she ran to find her place. The auditorium of Stoneybrook Academy was full. Each of the seats was taken. Every single student and teacher in the school was waiting to see Ms. Colman's class starring in *Alice in Wonderland*.

Leslie let the curtain fall into place. Then she ran to find Jannie. Jannie still was not talking to Leslie. But they had to perform together.

"Okay, I need Alice and the White Rabbit," Mrs. Morris said. "Karen and Sara, where are you two? It is time to find your places onstage."

Leslie watched as her mother led Karen and Sara to their places. In just a few moments, the curtains would open and the play would begin. Leslie felt the flutter of excitement again. Now that is just silly, she told herself. You are wearing a dopey costume. And soon you are going to have to play Tweedle*dee*. And dance around with Tweedle*dum*.

"Boys and girls and teachers," a voice called from the stage.

It was Ms. Colman.

The audience quieted down.

"Please get ready for our first performance of *Alice in Wonderland*! Our class has worked very hard on it. We hope you enjoy it."

The audience clapped their hands politely.

The curtain parted.

And Sara ran onstage, followed by Karen.

Leslie held her breath. No scenery fell

over. Sara and Karen remembered their lines. The audience was silent. They could not take their eyes off the stage. Slowly, Leslie let her breath out.

Leslie watched from backstage as Alice fell down the rabbit hole, met the Dormouse and the Caterpillar, went to the mad tea party, and chatted with the Cheshire Cat. Soon her mother was pushing her and Jannie toward the stage.

"Okay, Tweedledee and Tweedledum," said Mrs. Morris. "You're on."

To her surprise, Leslie felt nervous again. As she ran onto the stage she glanced at Jannie. Jannie looked terrified. Leslie was already holding Jannie's hand. Now she squeezed it. Jannie squeezed it back. So Leslie smiled at Jannie, and Jannie smiled back.

Tweedledee and Tweedledum began their song. The kids in the auditorium giggled. They liked the song! Leslie stopped feeling nervous. She was having

fun. Jannie was having fun, too.

When Leslie and Jannie ran offstage, the audience clapped.

Jannie grinned. "We were *good!*" she exclaimed.

"We were great!" said Leslie. Then she added, "Jannie? Are you talking to me again? Is our fight over?"

"Yes and yes," replied Jannie.

"I am sorry about all the things I did."

"That is okay. I am sorry about all the things I did."

"I am sorry I got mad at you."

"That is okay," said Leslie.

When *Alice in Wonderland* was over, the kids in Ms. Colman's class ran onto the stage. They took their bows in one long line.

"Bravo!" yelled the audience.

Leslie whispered to Jannie, "I cannot *wait* for our next performance."

About the Author

ANN M. MARTIN lives in New York and loves animals, especially cats. She has two cats of her own, Gussie and Woody.

Other books by Ann M. Martin that you might enjoy are *Rachel Parker, Kindergarten Show-Off* and the Baby-sitters Club series. She has also written the Baby-sitters Little Sister series starring Karen Brewer, one of the kids in Ms. Colman's class.

Ann grew up in Princeton, New Jersey, where she had many wonderful teachers like Ms. Colman. Ann likes ice cream, *I Love Lucy*, and especially sewing.

THE KIDS IN, MS. COLMAN'S CLASS

A new series by Ann M. Martin

Don't miss #4
SECOND GRADE BABY

"Hi, Ms. Colman," said Mrs. Springer. "I brought this for Natalie." Mrs. Springer held up a brown paper bag. "She forgot it this morning. It is her underwear. Her ballet lesson is this afternoon, and Natalie needs a change of clothes." Mrs. Springer waved to Natalie. Then she left.

Ms. Colman gave the bag to Natalie. Then she poked her head into the room next door.

Bobby grabbed the paper bag.

"I want to see Natalie's underwear!" he cried.

"Me, too!" shouted Hank.

Before Natalie knew it, every kid in her class had seen her underwear. And every kid had seen the name tags.

I am dead meat, said Natalie to herself.